THE TINY PERFECT
DINOSAUR
BOOK FOUR

Presenting Stegosaurus

by Jennifer Glossop with Dale Russell
Illustrated by Ely Kish

A SOMERVILLE HOUSE BOOK

ANDREWS AND McMEEL
A Universal Press Syndicate Company
Kansas City

Contents

This Is Stegosaurus 3
Two Kinds of Dinosaurs 4
Family Tree 6
The Biggest Stegosaur 8
How Are Fossils Made? 10
Stegosaurus Is Discovered.................................12
The Jurassic 14
The Mystery of the Plates..................................16
A Spiky Tail 18
Keeping Its Head Down 20
A Teeny, Tiny Brain 22
A Slow Eater 24
A Baby Without Plates 27
Stegosaurus's Neighbors 28
How Dinosaurs Became Extinct 30
Farewell to Stegosaurus 32

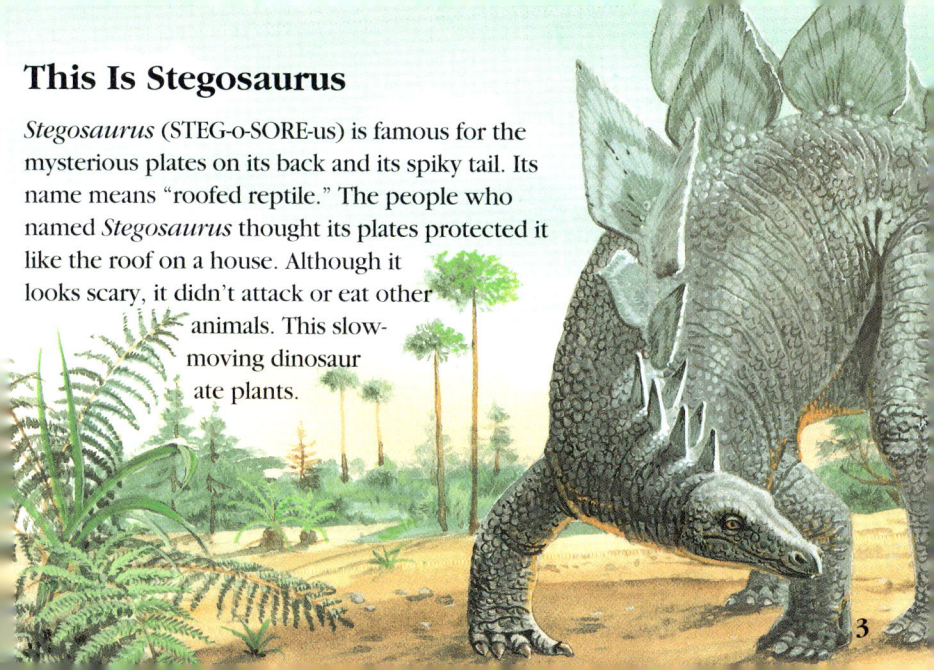

This Is Stegosaurus

Stegosaurus (STEG-o-SORE-us) is famous for the mysterious plates on its back and its spiky tail. Its name means "roofed reptile." The people who named *Stegosaurus* thought its plates protected it like the roof on a house. Although it looks scary, it didn't attack or eat other animals. This slow-moving dinosaur ate plants.

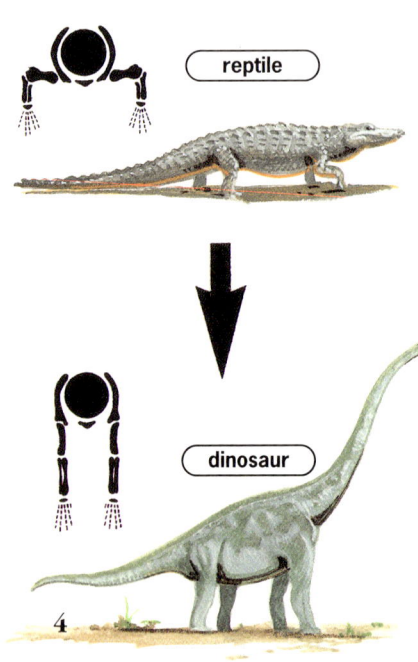

Two Kinds of Dinosaurs

About 200 million years ago, lots of animals lived on earth. One group of dog-sized reptiles called archosaurs (ARE-ko-saurs) had straighter legs than other reptiles. They looked a bit like modern crocodiles. Two main groups of dinosaurs evolved from these archosaurs.

The first group of dinosaurs had hip bones like those of lizards and crocodiles. They were called lizard-hipped dinosaurs, or saurischians (saw-RISH-i-ans). Eventually two groups of saurischians evolved: the two-legged meat-eaters like *Allosaurus* (AH-lo-SORE-us) and the long-necked plant-eaters like *Brachiosaurus* (BRAK-ee-o-SORE-us).

The second group of dinosaurs had hips similar in shape to those of modern birds. Although they are not related to birds, these dinosaurs are called bird-hipped dinosaurs, or ornithischians (OR-ni-THISH-i-ans). There were five groups of these plant-eating dinosaurs. *Stegosaurus* belongs to one of them — the stegosaurs, or plated dinosaurs.

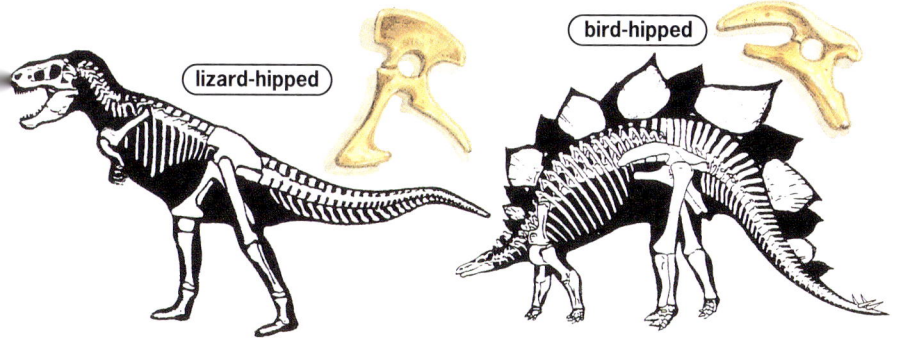

- flying reptiles
- ancestral archosaurs

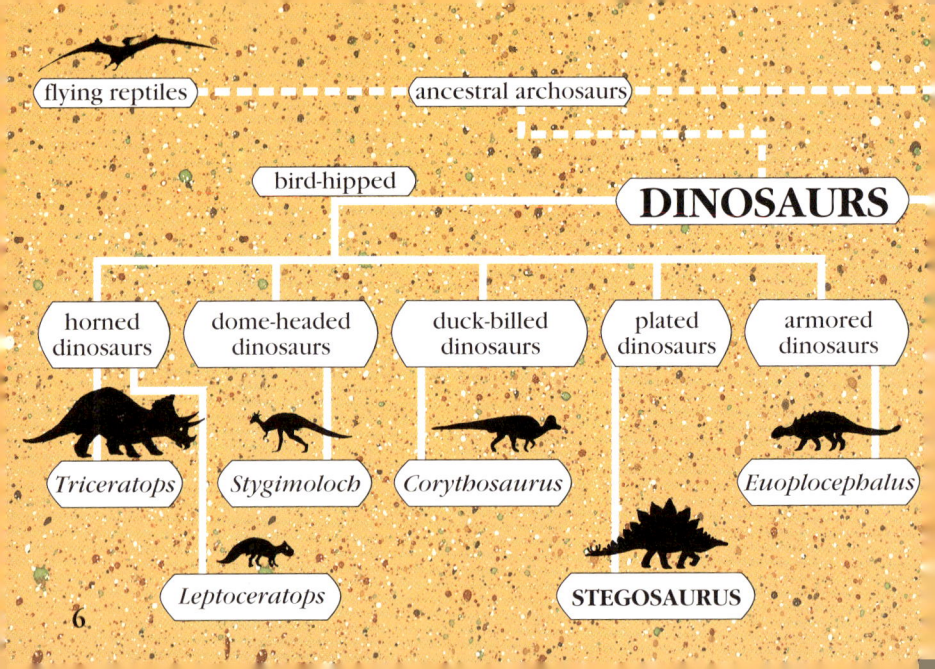

DINOSAURS

bird-hipped

- horned dinosaurs
  - *Triceratops*
  - *Leptoceratops*
- dome-headed dinosaurs
  - *Stygimoloch*
- duck-billed dinosaurs
  - *Corythosaurus*
- plated dinosaurs
  - **STEGOSAURUS**
- armored dinosaurs
  - *Euoplocephalus*

Family Tree

Paleontologists classify dinosaurs in many different groups. Here are some of the famous dinosaurs and the groups they belong in.

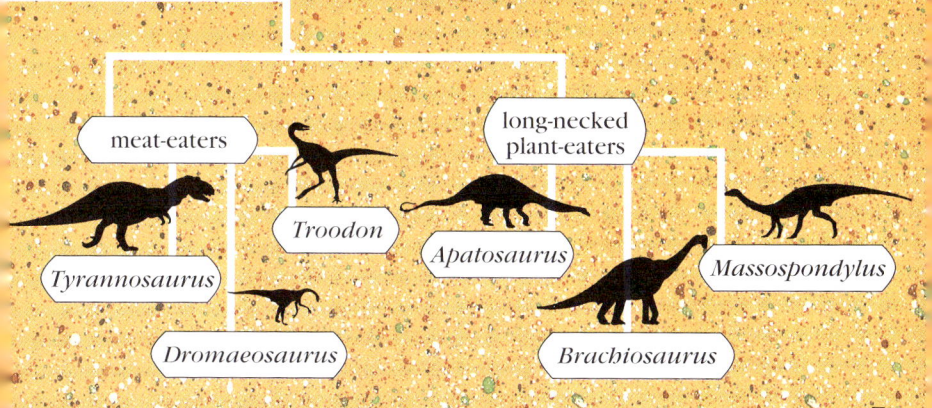

- crocodiles and alligators
- lizard-hipped
  - meat-eaters
    - *Tyrannosaurus*
    - *Troodon*
    - *Dromaeosaurus*
  - long-necked plant-eaters
    - *Apatosaurus*
    - *Brachiosaurus*
    - *Massospondylus*

The Biggest Stegosaur

Stegosaurus, the biggest of the stegosaurs, was about the size of a large van (fifteen feet or 4.5 meters long). It weighed four tons (3700 kg). The very tip of the highest plate on its back was eight feet (2.4 meters) above the ground.

Down its neck, back, and tail were two rows of bony plates. At the end of its tail were four bony spikes. It used the spikes to protect itself from other dinosaurs that wanted to eat it. One *Stegosaurus* would have been a big meal for several meat-eating dinosaurs like *Allosaurus*.

For such a big fellow, *Stegosaurus* had a very small head — about the size of a large dog's. Its brain was so small you could have held it in one hand.

9

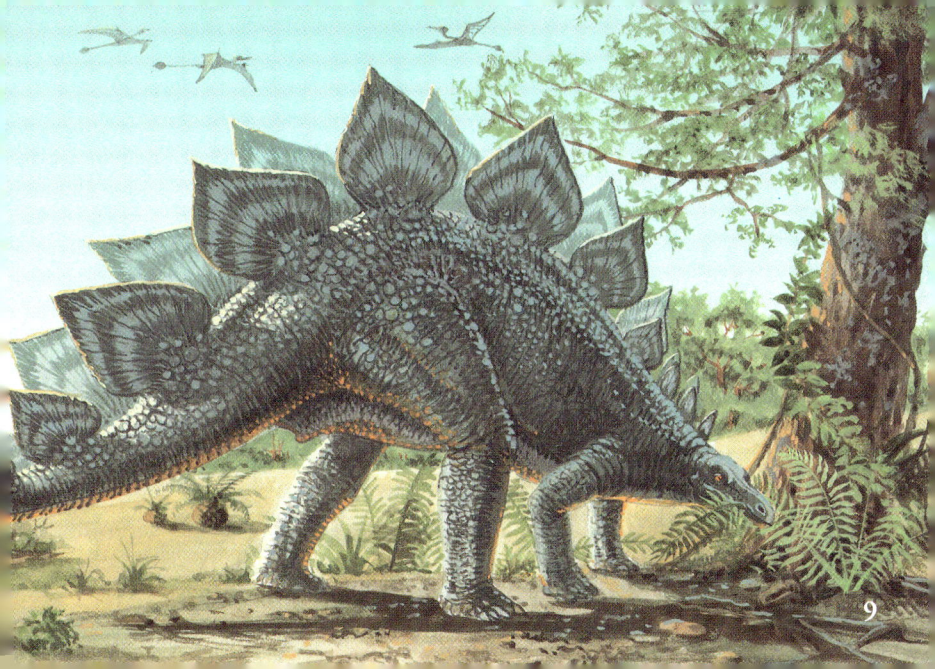

How Are Fossils Made?

Usually when animals die, even their bones decay after a few hundred years. How have some dinosaur bones lasted for millions of years?

Imagine an old, weak *Stegosaurus* going for a drink at a water hole. When he gets there, he finds the water hole has dried up. Starving, he falls down and dies.

Soon the rainy season starts. A flash flood covers the dinosaur's body with sand. The soft parts of his body rot away until only the bones are left. As more sand piles on top, minerals seep into the bones, and the sand around the bones hardens. Over many years both the sand and the bones turn to rock. The sand is now called sandstone, and the bones are called fossils.

Stegosaurus dies.

The rainy season brings a flash flood.

The bones turn to fossils.

The skeleton is discovered.

Stegosaurus Is Discovered

More than one hundred years ago, two American paleontologists (PAY-lee-on-TAW-lo-jists), scientists who study fossils, got into a race to see who could find the most dinosaur fossils. Othniel Charles Marsh and Edward Drinker Cope and their teams dug into rock formations in Colorado and Wyoming.

Each team worked furiously and guarded its secrets from the other. Soon they had found an amazing number of fossilized dinosaur skeletons.

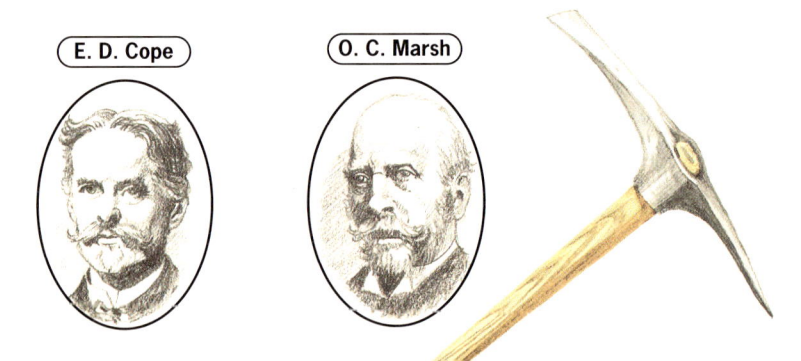

E. D. Cope

O. C. Marsh

Until that time, only nine dinosaur species had been discovered in North America. Between them, Marsh and Cope named more than one hundred new kinds, including *Stegosaurus*.

It was Marsh's team that unearthed the first *Stegosaurus* in 1877. They also discovered *Allosaurus* and *Triceratops* (try-SERR-a-tops).

Put together the bones that came with this book. (See the back of the poster for exact instructions.) You will have a skeleton of *Stegosaurus* like the one found by O. C. Marsh. The only difference is that on the model the plates are attached to the back so they don't fall off. On the actual fossils they were not attached to the backbone.

The Jurassic

Stegosaurus lived about 150 million years ago, at the end of a time called the Jurassic. The earth looked very different then. A map of the Jurassic world would show three continents, two smaller ones in the north and a giant one in the south. Rivers, shallow lakes, and seas flowed over the land.

During the Jurassic, there were two seasons: a hot, dry season and a warm, rainy season. It never snowed.

In swampy areas, ferns and horsetails grew. In other, better drained areas, there were forests of cypresses, ginkgoes, and cycads, a short, palmlike plant. Plant-eating dinosaurs had lots and lots to eat. Some — especially the long-necked dinosaurs like *Brachiosaurus* — ate leaves from the tops of trees as giraffes do today. Others, like *Stegosaurus*, browsed closer to the ground. While these big dinosaurs munched away, bits of leaves often dropped out of their mouths. Smaller dinosaurs scurried about, gobbling up the dropped leaves. Wherever the plant-eaters found their dinner, they had to be alert for the meat-eating hunters, who preyed on them.

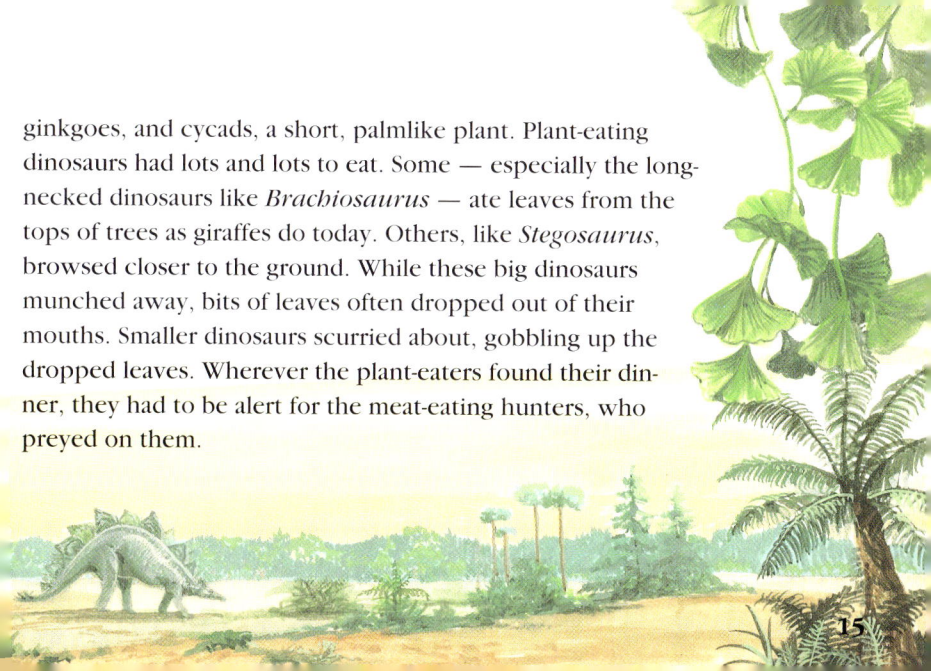

The Mystery of the Plates

At first, scientists thought *Stegosaurus*'s huge plates protected it from other dinosaurs. But although the plates were strong and solid, they weren't hard and tough on the outside. They were covered with skin and filled with blood vessels. Soon scientists began to wonder if the plates were used for other things. Maybe they helped scare away other animals. After all, the plates made *Stegosaurus* look bigger. Or maybe a male *Stegosaurus* used its plates to attract a female. Perhaps the plates on the males were a different color than those on the females.

Most scientists now believe the plates helped *Stegosaurus* stay warm or cool off. In cool weather, *Stegosaurus* turned so its plates faced the sun. The blood vessels inside the plates carried the sun's warmth to the rest of its body. On hot days, the dinosaur could cool off by turning so its plates caught a breeze and gave off body heat.

There is another mystery about *Stegosaurus*'s plates. How were they arranged? Although the plates lined the backbone, or spine, they were firmly attached to skin, not bone. After *Stegosaurus* died, the plates fell off, making it hard to tell how they were arranged. Many scientists thought they were lined up side by side in pairs. But since an alternating pattern is better for cooling, this seems more likely.

in pairs?

?

alternating?

✓

A Spiky Tail

Animals that snuck up behind *Stegosaurus* were in for a nasty shock. At the end of *Stegosaurus*'s tail were four special plates that looked like spikes. Unlike the other plates, these were not covered with flesh. *Stegosaurus* used these bony spines to defend itself. With one wag of its strong tail, it would have sent its enemies flying.

Stegosaurus looked much the same from each end. Perhaps more than one meat-eater, thinking it was going for *Stegosaurus*'s throat, got a painful surprise when it encountered a spiked tail.

19

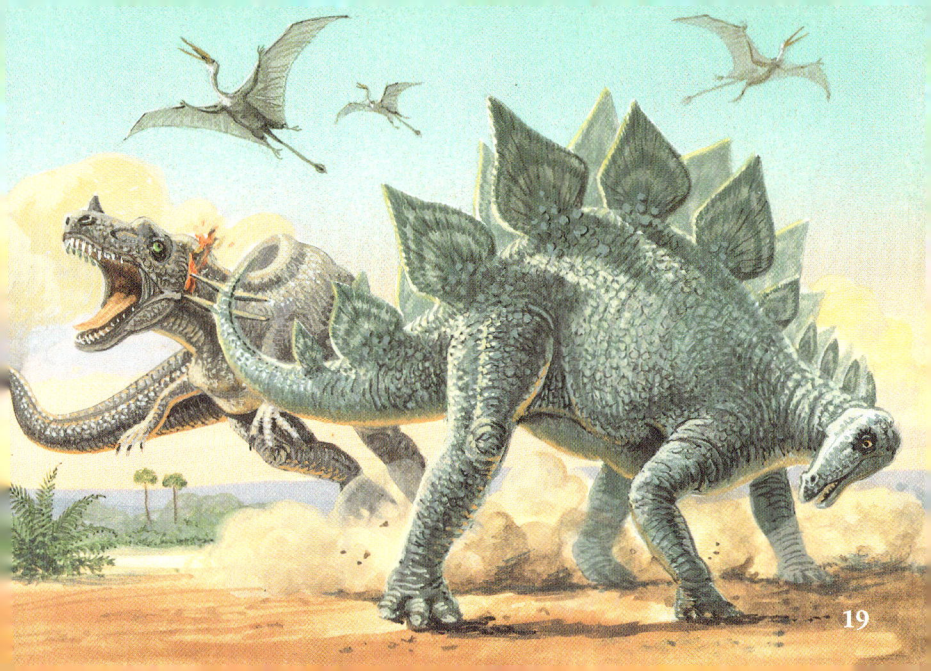

Keeping Its Head Down

Stegosaurus had to keep its head down. It didn't have much choice. Its hind legs were twice as long as its front legs, making it tallest at the hips.

All bird-hipped dinosaurs have longer back legs, and scientists think that many of them walked on two feet. But from *Stegosaurus*'s legs and feet we can tell that it spent most of its time on all fours. Its legs were heavy and strong to support its weight. And its front

Hypsilophodon

feet were shaped somewhat like an elephant's. It had short, strong toes and hooflike nails. In comparison, another bird-hipped dinosaur, *Hypsilophodon* (hip-si-LOF-o-don), had slimmer legs and its feet were built for running.

Was *Stegosaurus* able to lift itself up on its hind legs like a bear? Not often! If it ever did, it would only have been to scare away enemies or to reach a tasty leaf.

elephant foot

Stegosaurus foot

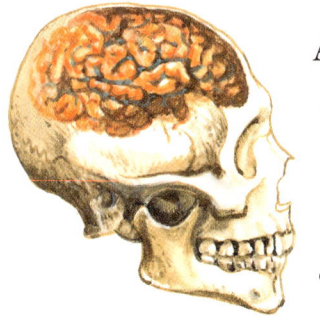

A Teeny, Tiny Brain

Poor *Stegosaurus*! Everyone thinks it must have been the stupidest of dinosaurs because it had such a tiny brain. But since it survived on earth for millions of years — much longer than humans have so far — it must have been smart enough to take care of itself.

For a while it was thought that *Stegosaurus* had a second brain to make up for the small one in its head. This brain was supposed to be in spaces in the hip region, which were much bigger than the brain area in its skull. No one believes this theory any more, however. It's more likely that these spaces contained thicker nerves that helped *Stegosaurus* control its tail and back legs. Or they could have stored fat and sugar for times when the dinosaur needed extra energy.

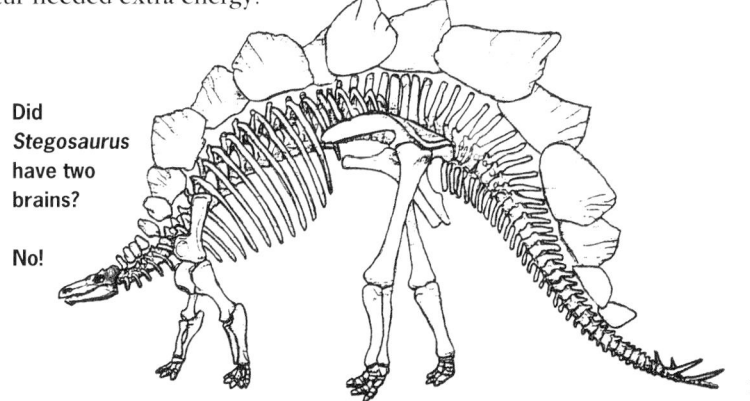

Did *Stegosaurus* have two brains?

No!

A Slow Eater

Stegosaurus probably lived on the edges of the flatlands created when rivers overflowed during the rainy season. Groups of *Stegosaurus* moved around in herds, as bison do. They spent most of their time eating to provide fuel for their big bodies.

Stegosaurus was a slow eater. It didn't have sharp front teeth to bite off its food. Instead, like other bird-hipped dinosaurs, it had a small, horny beak in the front of its skull. Along the sides of its jaws, it had leaf-shaped teeth, which it used to chop up plants. Its weak jaw muscles weren't much help either. Even if *Stegosaurus* chose only the tenderest leaves, chewing its food took a long time.

25

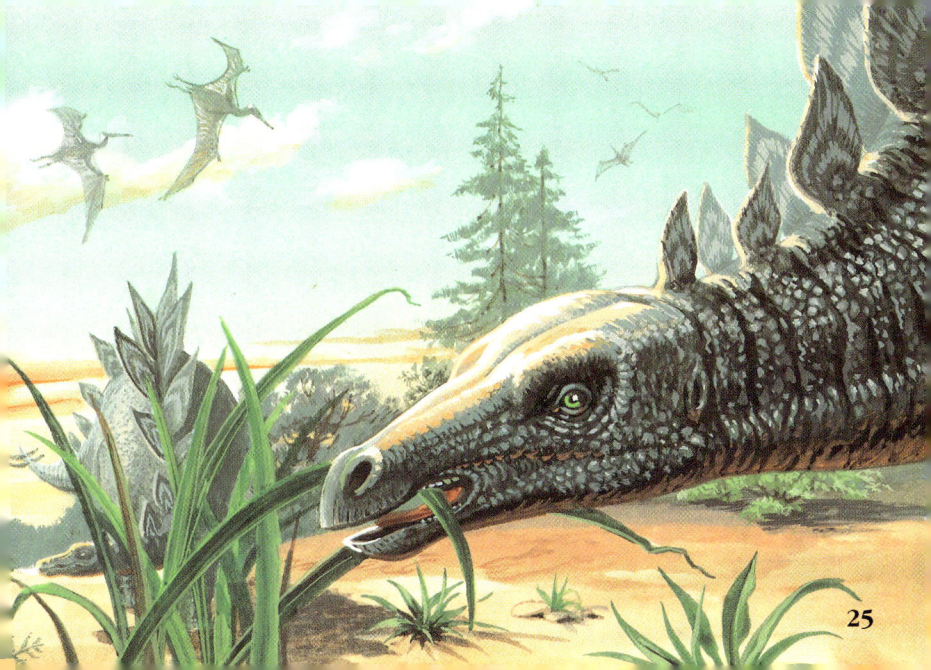

Did *Stegosaurus* look after its young? We don't know for sure.

A Baby Without Plates

Like other reptiles and modern birds, dinosaurs laid hard-shelled eggs. Scientists have found some fossilized dinosaur eggs and some fossils of infant dinosaurs, including a young *Stegosaurus* about the size of a large dog.

There were no plates on this young *Stegosaurus.* They could be missing, but it's also possible that a *Stegosaurus* didn't grow plates until it was older, in the same way that moose grow antlers, or men grow beards.

We don't know how many eggs *Stegosaurus* laid at a time, or even if the parents stayed around to see their youngsters hatch. It certainly seems unlikely that *Stegosaurus* parents would have sat on a nest to keep the eggs warm. They would have crushed them.

After the babies hatched, they probably had to look after themselves. The young dinosaurs may have eaten insects and small animals, as well as plants. They may even have eaten their own eggshells. Eggshells are made of calcium, which helps bones grow strong.

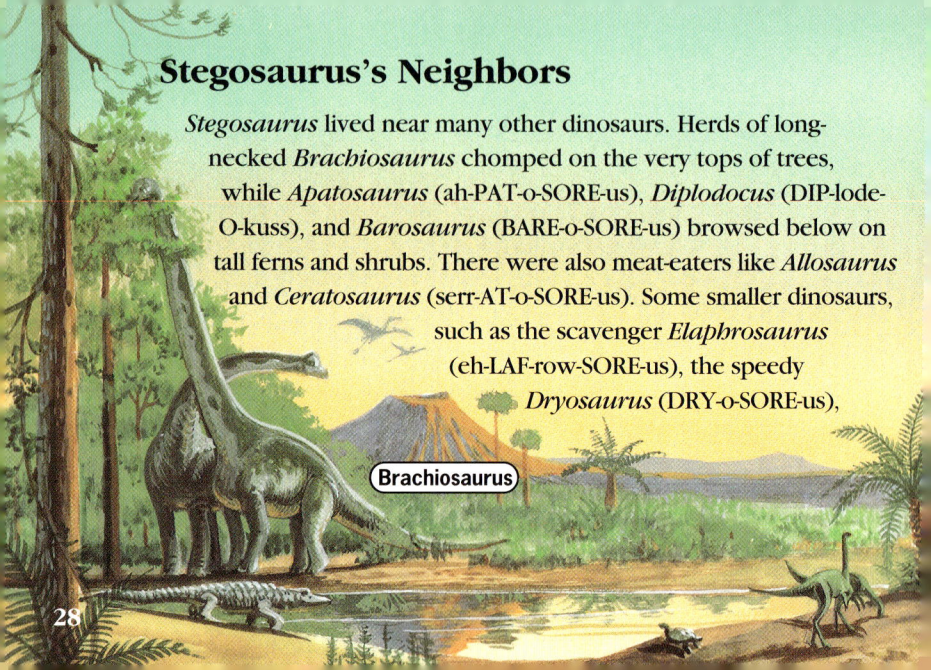

Stegosaurus's Neighbors

Stegosaurus lived near many other dinosaurs. Herds of long-necked *Brachiosaurus* chomped on the very tops of trees, while *Apatosaurus* (ah-PAT-o-SORE-us), *Diplodocus* (DIP-lode-O-kuss), and *Barosaurus* (BARE-o-SORE-us) browsed below on tall ferns and shrubs. There were also meat-eaters like *Allosaurus* and *Ceratosaurus* (serr-AT-o-SORE-us). Some smaller dinosaurs, such as the scavenger *Elaphrosaurus* (eh-LAF-row-SORE-us), the speedy *Dryosaurus* (DRY-o-SORE-us),

Brachiosaurus

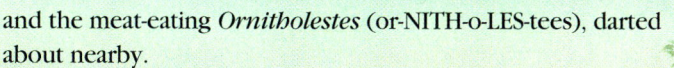

and the meat-eating *Ornitholestes* (or-NITH-o-LES-tees), darted about nearby.

The ancestors of animals that are still around today lived then. Small crocodiles scurried through the brush; frogs, lizards, and turtles sunned themselves; and dragonflies skimmed through the air. Small, primitive mammals crept about at night.

How Dinosaurs Became Extinct

By the end of the Jurassic, many kinds of dinosaurs, including *Stegosaurus*, had become extinct. Some stegosaurs lived on into the next great age, the Cretaceous. But when that time period ended about 65 million years ago, all dinosaurs had vanished from the earth.

No one knows what killed the last of the dinosaurs, but many scientists think a comet that struck the earth caused enormous changes around the world. The impact would have created thick dust that blocked out the sun. Plants would have died, and without plants, the plant-eating dinosaurs would have starved to death. The meat-eaters would have followed soon. Lots of chemicals would also have been thrown into the air, causing acid rain, which would have further harmed plants and animals.

31

Farewell to Stegosaurus

Stegosaurus was the biggest of the many plated dinosaurs. It roamed the earth for about 10 million years. From the time its fossilized bones were discovered, this peaceful and slow-moving animal has been a favorite of everybody who likes and studies dinosaurs.

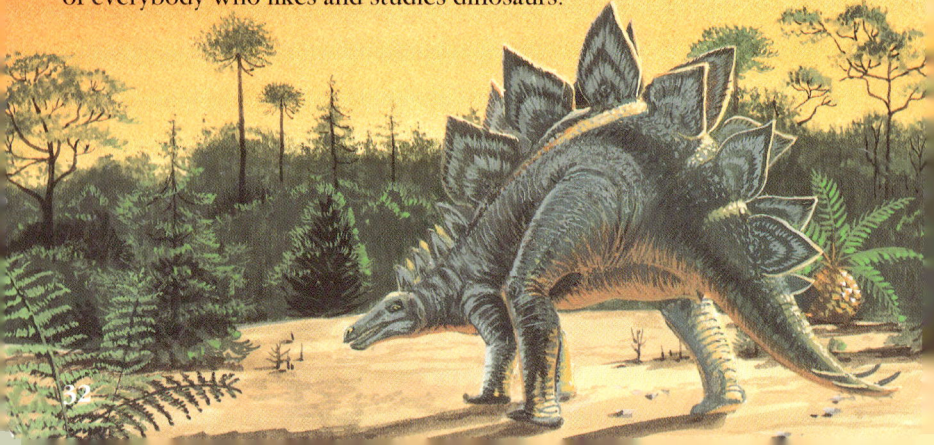